GW00363433

MAKING
Love

THIS BOOK presents the tantric teachings of one of the spiritual masters of our time. Barry Long's teaching on love has transformed the lives of thousands of men and women around the world.

'This book presents a radical concept . . . if only the world would learn to really make love, major change would be wrought.' LIVING NOW MAGAZINE

'This book is not your average book on lovemaking. It's about making love in its purest form and highest purpose. It's a programme of lessons for committed lovers looking for a way to truly make love tangible, by learning how to love honestly and completely.
Long's no nonsense approach openly addresses the many misconceptions around our sexuality, challenging current erroneous beliefs prevalent in society that actually make us less rather than more loving.' GOLDEN AGE

'If you are willing to have some of your most romantic and emotional dreams shattered, they will be replaced with an understanding of the divinity of love, the purity and fulfilment of love in a way that is unique in my experience. If you are sincere in your search for yourself, for love, for the divine, then the cool clarity of this volume will inform, enlighten and challenge you.' NOVA HOLISTIC JOURNAL

Also by Barry Long

Knowing Yourself

To Woman In Love

Only Fear Dies

Meditation A Foundation Course

Stillness Is The Way

Wisdom and Where To Find It

Raising Children in Love, Justice and Truth

The Origins of Man and the Universe

MAKING
Love

SEXUAL LOVE
THE DIVINE WAY

BARRY LONG

BARRY LONG BOOKS

This text first published 1998

Barry Long's 'Making Love' first recorded on audio cassette 1984

The present revised text re-recorded 1995

Also published on audio cassette

BARRY LONG BOOKS

BCM Box 876, London WC1N 3XX, England

Box 5277, Gold Coast MC, Qld 4217, Australia

6230 Wilshire Boulevard Suite 251, Los Angeles, CA 90048, USA

© Barry Long 1984, 1995, 1998

The right of Barry Long to be identified as the author of this work
has been asserted in accordance with sections 77 and 78
of the Copyright Designs and Patents Act 1988

All rights reserved. No part of this book may be reproduced,
stored in a retrieval system or transmitted in any form or by any
means without the prior permission of the publisher

Cataloguing in Publication Data:

A catalogue record for this book is available from The British Library

Library of Congress Catalog Card Number: 98-91353

ISBN 1 899324 14 3

(Barry Long Audio ISBN 1 899324 02 X)

Front cover photo: Silvia Rivas

Photo of Barry Long: Ambyr Johnston

Printed in England on acid-free paper by Biddles Ltd

CONTENTS

ABOUT BARRY LONG

*B*arry Long is an Australian who speaks to a worldwide audience about the truth of life and love. One of the spiritual masters of our time, his teaching not only encompasses the whole of human experience but extends to the most profound reaches of consciousness. Yet many would say his outstanding contribution to their everyday lives has been his teaching on sexual love.

Barry Long's spiritual awakening began in 1957 when he was 31 and a happily married family man with a successful career in journalism. His love of God was so intense it fired an inner crisis of extreme emotional pain. Eventually he met a woman and loved her with such intensity that love of God and love of woman became one. A vision revealed to him that she, his divine beloved, the Woman in all women, was God.

During the next twenty years Barry Long's spiritual realisations continued and he began to attract students. In the 1980's they came to him in increasing numbers and he became well known as an outspoken and uncompromising teacher, first in England and later in Australia.

Throughout 1990-1993 he travelled the world giving many seminars in Europe and America. Within the context of his broader teaching he addressed the fundamental issues of lack of love and sexual unhappiness, teaching man and woman to get their partnerships right by being honest with each other. Cutting to the core of the problem, his compassion and practical common sense helped many couples to make a new start, together or separately.

All this time Barry Long's love of woman has remained constant. She is always by his side. Through deep and lasting partnerships he has made his realisation of love real in the midst of everyday living. It is this realised knowledge of divine love that we meet in this book.

It is a radical teaching and not always easy; but by the testimony of the many who've been before you, the changes it brings are those you long for. This is tantric teaching of the highest degree, introduced to our tangled relationships so that woman might be the love she really is, and man more worthy of her.

INTRODUCTION

The text of this book was written to be recorded as two audio tapes in the English language. The first release was in 1984. The second release in 1995 included some additions because my teaching had moved on, as love always moves on. The tapes have been helpful to many thousands of men and women in many countries. I'm told they have been copied and distributed far more widely than I know. Although they are used by many therapists I have never been associated with any other teacher or teaching. I do not endorse any sexual teachings other than my own. Nor do I endorse anyone teaching in my name or who says they have been inspired by my tapes. The tapes and this book are for the individual man and woman to put into practice and are not intended for others to teach from. All real teachers in love draw only on their own inspiration and experience.

As important as lovemaking is to my teaching, it is not all that I teach. To make love rightly requires a sincere and genuine endeavour to live the truth in all the other aspects of your life. For example, it is necessary to start getting the external circumstances of your life right because if you are troubled by some relationship or situation, you will be unable to reach the degree of stillness within that right lovemaking requires. Lovemaking is not just about making physical love, it is about making your love and life trouble free.

This book is a comprehensive basis for divine lovemaking between man and woman. Please use it to dismantle your sexual greed and frustration and start to discover love as it really is, and not as you think it is or want it to be.

Barry Long

THE PURPOSE

I teach man and woman how to be true to love and how to be honest in their relationships. I help them to discover a divine love beyond all sexual imagining. The key to the mystery of divine love is to see love as it is, and not as you think you know it or like to imagine it.

This book is for partners who yearn to reach the truth of love in themselves and each other. By attentively reading what I have to say, and then practising it patiently and steadfastly over the months and years ahead, you and your partner can discover a more real, a more divine love. It is not easy to get it right and sometimes you may even feel it's a hopeless task, but by reading this book you will always be reminded that your love has purpose.

Without purpose love *is* hopeless, as you already know, or you would not be reading this now. As you can see in the world around you, love on this planet is in a dreadful mess. But in this book I am going to show you the purpose of love and your individual place in love or life on earth.

The cause of most of the unhappiness on earth is that man and woman have actually forgotten how to make physical love. This is the greatest tragedy of all time. The forgetfulness has been going on and slowly getting worse for so many thousands of years, that it's now a tragedy for the whole of mankind. This means that only the individual man or woman has any chance of starting to correct it. There can be no mass solutions. The problem is too personal and too deep. Everybody has to do it for himself or herself, or it can't be done.

I suggest you read this book again and again. Each time you will have new insights into love.

DIVINE LOVE AND HUMAN LOVE

*W*oman's basic unhappiness, her perennial discontent, is because man can no longer reach her physically. Her emotional excess, depressions, tearful frustration, even premenstrual tension and the conditions leading to hysterectomy and other uterine problems, are due to man's sexual failure to gather or release in lovemaking her finest, fundamental, female energies. These extraordinarily beautiful divine energies are intense and exquisite and when left untapped in woman, as they are now, they degenerate into psychic or emotional disturbances, and eventually crystallise into physical abnormalities. The womb gives birth to all things.

Man's basic unhappiness, his perennial restlessness, is because in forgetting how to make love he's abandoned his original divine authority and lost sexual control of himself. His emotional or psychic degeneracy manifests as sex obsession. All men, without exception, are sex obsessed. This means compulsive sexual fantasising, chronic masturbation (even when living with a partner), sex repression leading to anger and violence, and the universal symptoms of chasing wealth and getting lost in work. Busy-ness and wealth-gathering compensate for being an inept lover and are cover-ups (in both sexes) for the inability or fear to love. Because of his neglect of love — neglect of woman — man suffers from premature ejaculation, guilt, anxiety, self-doubt, impotence, sexual atrophy masquerading as sexual disinterest, sexual abstinence due to repressed fear of failure, sexual bravado and lack of true wisdom — all of which he inflicts on woman, aggravating her basic discontent and his own restlessness.

No matter how much a woman loves her man and wants to give her love to him, she will not and cannot give up all her divine energies if he is not yet himself, fully integrated or aligned with love. As very few men are themselves, the gap of unhappiness between man and woman keeps on growing.

To be a fully integrated male, a man has to assimilate in his body the divine female energies that woman can only release to him through right physical lovemaking. But the man has to be man enough. He has to be able to love her enough; that is, love her divinely or selflessly during the actual act of lovemaking. He has to be able to absorb and express sufficient love in his body to reach the highest part of her, and love enough to extract the divine energies from her deepest centre. To be able to love in this way is the authority man has lost — his only true authority over woman.

This requires pure love. It does not depend on technique. A man may develop his sexual technique but he cannot use expertise to make divine love. Exciting sensations and orgasms are gratifying and give him a form of authority, but they are not the love that woman craves. He may satisfy her, like a good meal. But soon she hungers again and eventually despises her appetite or herself, because she knows she is not being loved.

Man has failed to serve love and failed physically to serve woman, who is the personification of love. The penalty for man is woman's tyrannous emotionality. Wherever he loves, or tries to love, she will one day shock him, stun him, devastate him by suddenly revealing herself as the fiendess, the living female demon of emotion.

The fiendess shows herself when he is attached and can't just walk away. A man who has not yet experienced the hatred of the fiendess has not yet experienced love. A woman who has not yet seen herself being the fiendess has not yet connected with her love.

To man, the fiendess of emotion in woman is hell on earth. This is the part of her he cannot handle or understand. The demon of his own failure to love comes to life to scorn, abuse and torment him. He is terrified of it. He bluffs and blusters his way through. But finally, as he grows old in the relationship and gives up for the sake of some peace, the fiendess will conquer him and force him to surrender the last vestige of his manliness and authority. Then they both grow old together, feeling safe, but half dead as they lean on each other in the awful world of compromise.

While the world continues as it is, the fiendess will not allow man to forget his failure to love woman rightly. Woman must be loved. The future of the human race depends on woman being loved because only when woman is truly loved can man be truly himself and regain his lost authority. Only then can peace return to earth. Yet woman as she is now cannot be loved for long (or for good) by man as he is now. Together they are trapped in a vicious circle and if left to their own ideas of love, there is no way out for them.

∞

At the beginning of time, when the world had just begun, the state of man and woman was very different. The beginning of time and the world is relatively recent compared with the beginning of the universe or the earth. The earth is not the world. The world was built by man. The world began about 12,000 years ago when man identified for the first time with physical death. At this point time began, providing the sense of tomorrow and continuity on which the world is built. Before this there was only past — extending back to the first life forms. And before life on earth, there was neither time nor past. There was only the present, the presence or the timeless. Time is not a process of things getting better. Time is the process of things getting worse. And things have got a lot worse for man and woman and their love since they started to slip into time and self-forgetfulness, around 10,000 B.C.

You might say this sounds like myth. It is myth, but not myth as 'fable' or 'fiction'. What I'm going to describe is the truth. True myth is the only means we have left of communicating the truth — the original state of man and woman on earth. So please be as still and receptive as you can. Suspend your critical mind while I outline for you the myth or truth of man and woman — your own original state, which you are striving to regain by loving and living in time today.

Around 12,000 years ago the individual bodies of man and woman were permanently surrounded by a magnificent, golden orb or halo. Radiating out from the solar plexus, it extended visibly above the head, into the ground and beyond the reach of the outstretched arms. The woman's orb was a slightly deeper gold than the man's. But both had the same dazzling, sublime and beauteous quality.

Woman was pure love; the serene, passive pole of human spiritual love on earth. Man, the active and positive pole, was also love but not pure love in the same sense. His love was a pure authority; the masculine principle which was the guardian of love or woman on earth. He or his love was responsible for maintaining the golden divine quality of love between man and woman. The brilliance of their orbs or halos at any time reflected the intensity and purity of that love.

Their physical lovemaking was ecstatic. The divine energy generated was so powerful that after making love their radiant bodies or halos blazed with incredible splendour. This self-luminous radiance of spirit or love created in each by physical union was the manifestation of their godhead on earth. For man and woman at the beginning of time were gods, and they sustained the awareness and presence of their godhead, their time-lessness, by making divine physical love.

The halo, the golden energy, was their means of communication, whether together or apart. Its range went far beyond the visible outline, and through it each was in constant undisturbed touch with the other, in silence and stillness, in mutual consciousness of pure love — God.

When either halo needed new energy, man and woman would draw together and make love, make God. As the only two conscious physical poles of love on earth they would illuminate and energise themselves. He would regenerate her love, while she would restore his love and authority. Communication between them was so complete there was no need for speech. Speaking developed with time. It developed when men and women started to forget to love and began to lose themselves in time given to other things, to building the world. Thus men and women forgot how to be themselves all the time; and as they failed to make divine physical love, their halos, their consciousness, lost the golden God-connection. They had to start talking across the developing gap between them. And then in the distance of speech arose misunderstanding and emotion. As time or lovelessness invaded the bodies of man and woman, speech replaced the immediacy and fullness of love. Vocabulary grew and grew. Instead of *being* love, they declared 'I love you'. And there developed many wordy substitutes for love.

The intensity of the halo was retained in some individuals longer than in others but with time or the past increasing in everybody, things got inexorably worse. In a few thousand years most men and women had completely forgotten how to make love and to be love. Although apparently performing the same physical act, they were unable to release or generate divine energy or personify in themselves the living spirit or presence of love, the timeless. Their bodies, no longer aligned in love, were aligned in time and emotion. Instead of making pure love they made emotional, demanding love, and instead of producing spiritually enlightened children, they produced emotionally dependent ones.

Woman was now confused and perennially discontented. Man, having lost his authority, was now impatient with her; and in trying to find a substitute for his authority he became perennially busy and restless. Lacking the authority to control her, he used his superior physical and economic strength to force her into an inferior social position, particularly by exploiting her love of her young. This so enraged her that it engendered the fiendess, who as long as time continued would never forget or forgive his injustice and corruption of love.

The human race, the race into time, had begun.

⁕

A few men and women retained some ability to love divinely within themselves by deliberately not making physical love. These were the mystics, saints and ascetics. They turned their attention inward and loved the divine energies in their own bodies. By refusing to mate with other bodies (now filling with time and emotion in the form of discontent and restlessness) they kept themselves relatively pure; but it was a pale and lop-sided purity, measured against the full, rich original radiance. Denying the earthly need of union with the opposite sex, the saintly alternative was fundamentally exclusive, unnatural and selfish — despite its lofty devotion and idealism. Consequently it produced half-integrated and only partly divine men and women.

Things were getting unmistakably worse. The result was reflected in the orbs and halos which had gradually shrunk in size and illumination to a small circle of light around the head. You see this today depicted in old paintings and icons, particularly of Christian saints. These shrunken, miniature halos show just how restricted and formalised man's idea of love on earth had become. By excluding the whole of his or her body from divine union with the opposite sex, and grounding love solely in the abstraction of the mind, the halo was reduced to circle the head alone; or at best, the upper part of the body.

The adoption of celibacy by the mystics was a great tragedy for mankind. Mystics and saints just might have saved the day, or the world, had they acted more selflessly. It could be said that due to the inrush of time they had no choice. At least in their way they managed to keep some pure divine love on earth — until saint-hood itself all but disappeared under the weight of time. But the truth is that they didn't love enough. They didn't love their fellow man and woman with sufficient golden intensity to dip into the divine mind in their own bodies through intercourse. Making love to give guidance or an inspired example was too much of a self-sacrifice.

Despite their divine love, and swamped by time like the rest of mankind, the mystics and saints had com-pletely forgotten how to make physical love. But they didn't realise it. And they were very emotional about it. They even made a virtue of their forgetfulness. This is particularly evident by the time the Christian Church appeared. In their relentless passion, perplexed and ridden by guilt, Christian saints denounced physical lovemaking. Like the mob that screamed 'Crucify him!' they condemned the love they feared and did not under-stand. Or they remained aloof. Although compassionate and mindful of the peripheral sufferings of mankind — the poverty, disease and violence — they always dodged the central issue of physical love, the cause of most of the unhappiness on earth including their own. Even Jesus, if we are to believe his priests, avoided the issue completely and left not one word of guidance for men and women whose tireless preoccupation, now as then, is the attempt to make physical love. Because of the glaring omission of sexuality from his teachings, the Messiah has a lot to answer for — if you believe his priests and interpreters.

Saintly men and women have burdened everyone in the West with their own awful guilt and the notion that making physical love is a sin to burn in hell for. How many billions of innocent boys and girls and men and women have suffered the hell on earth of sexual guilt, and still do, because of the Christian saints' lack of courage to love? 'God make me celibate — but not today', prayed Saint Augustine. Why didn't he ask God to show him why he loved woman so much that he couldn't stay away from her, instead of praying for an intellectual ideal that just wasn't true?

So the Christians, their saints, and all the celibate monks, ascetics and devotees of all religions who turned away from physical love tried to keep their hands clean — out of the real muck of love where ordinary men and women have to live. 'God is enough', they said. But is that true, if you're not a saint? Is it true for you? Or do you long to make love . . . and perhaps sense something divine, pure and godly in making love, which you know must be there and must be found?

Love is needed here on earth and it starts between you and me, man and woman. We cannot opt out of the reality of love on earth and put love in some other place, some heaven. Love is not needed by God, who in that other place is the source of love. If you want to escape to God in your love, and leave man and woman behind, then God help you. You will never be complete. Man and woman need the God of love in the thick of it, here on earth, not somewhere else where it already is and they are not. Only you and I together can make that love, that God, here. It is the lack of love or lack of God between us that has brought the world today to the brink of annihilation by its own hand.

Where is the origin of all love on earth, even the love of God, if not in making love? For is not everyone, even the other-worldly saint, born of lovemaking?

Is it intelligent to ignore the possibility that the sweetest natural physical sensation two human beings can produce together on earth signifies a reality? Isn't that the obvious place to start looking for a divine love?

Have you been told to 'love God'? No one on earth can possibly love God by an act of his or her own will. How can you love if you don't love? What would you say if I said 'Feel hungry!' when you weren't hungry?

Or perhaps you've been told to 'love everybody'. How can you love everybody? Can you possibly do it, really? Is everybody so lovable?

Do you really love your enemies? Did you tell your children today (not last Christmas) to love those who beat or bully them? Today when someone crosses you, see if you love him.

Let's be straight. Let's be honest with ourselves. We would all love to love everyone. But could we please just start with our partner?

Perhaps you say: 'Love everyone in spite of the natural tendency to be unloving. That's the task.' There is no task, no duty, no hardship in love. To try to love as a task is to follow the shameful, guilt-ridden, other-worldly way. That is not the way to love.

You start to love by making love. Which is what you and everyone else on earth most want to do anyway. But you must learn how to make love rightly; that is, without self-indulgence, without seeking emotional satisfaction and self-gratification.

Breaking the sexual habits and appetites of a lifetime will take some time and a lot of love. It will not be easy. But you will know by the feeling of rightness that you are on the way back to a more real, more fulfilling love. Eventually, after you have learned to make true physical love and have started to restore your golden halo, you'll find you have discovered how to love your fellow man and how to love God.

Woman has learned to make love through man who does not know how to make love. Hence the dreadful mess that love is in. Since time began she has been manipulated and encouraged to feel that the finest expression of her love is to please men sexually. The truth is the other way round. The finest expression of love is to have man delight her sexually. This he can only do when he can forget his preoccupation with orgasm and excitement and be sufficiently selfless or present in love to collect and receive her divine energies. For him, these are the finest expression of her love.

By teaching her to please him and satisfy him down through the ages, man has taught woman to want him and to project herself sexually to make herself exciting to him. He addicted her to an emotional and physical craving for his sexual attention. And he did this by neglecting to love her.

Woman had no affirmation of love, her true nature, since there was no man to love her rightly. So she settled for sexual excitation, which men had persuaded her was love. Men addicted her to this by teaching her that there is no purpose to physical love outside of making babies or selfish pleasure.

Man in his selfishness taught woman to be selfish. He taught her to excite him physically whenever love was not present; to project herself sexually for their mutual entertainment, through clothing, make-up, dance and posing. And he encouraged her to let him excite her (and himself) through digital stimulation of her clitoris to the point of orgasm, instead of loving the beauty of her whole body.

The loveless narcotic of sex numbed her and like all addictions, engendered fear — fear of losing him or his attention, and fear of other women in the form of jealousy and female competition. If she didn't satisfy him another woman soon would. And with this went the intimidating thought sown in her by all her sexual partners, that if she didn't comply she'd be left all alone.

As a reaction to this male infamy woman discovered cunt power — the power to tease man and manipulate him without delivering the goods, or by denying the goods when he wanted them. But the spell of cunt power, being largely imaginary, soon wore off after she let him enter her body. He would soon tire of her and go off with another woman.

Woman's subconscious dependence on the fluctuating sexual attention of men rules her choice of partner. She may go for either an exciting man whom she thinks she can control, or an agreeable and safe partner whom she can quietly bend to her wants. Both kinds of partnership usually end — either in disaster, or boredom and indifference.

Male sexuality is put into woman in sexual intercourse, and because it is substantive, it stays on in her. Its effect is a periodic wispy shadow of depression that she can't explain but accepts as normal. It clouds her perception, making her feel emotional and not herself. The same male sexuality is the active outgoing selfish drive which made the world a violent and loveless place. In woman, this destructive shadow of man subtly influences her choice of a partner. So very seldom is he Mr. Right. The male shadow in her is doubt. And it is the shadow that chooses. While woman wants the right to choose she has to make a choice; and then she must live with the shadow, doubt, in the man and in herself.

Woman in her natural state is not dependent on man. She loves him. And in love there is no dependence, no attachment, and no fear of losing. She is the passive, attracting principle. She is an irresistible living magnet. She draws to herself a right man to love her truly and divinely. There's no choice in it.

For woman today to return to her natural golden state takes time. But having suffered enough from man's sexuality she gradually learns not to compromise where there is not enough love. Finally this brings her a man who can remove the shadow from woman who is his love.

A woman is only ever less than her true nature because of man's lack of love. She went off into her dream to escape his sexuality. Her babies have long been a substitute for his love. Unlike man, a real woman can exist without sexual intercourse or masturbation. She waits for love, not sex. Woman only lusts for man when she identifies with the male sexuality he has induced in her. 'Nymphomania' is a male invention and fantasy projection, like sex-shops, pornography and prostitution, all kept going by male sexuality and lack of love in all concerned.

Woman has been utterly fooled by man, pathologically brainwashed. And as modern woman congratulates herself on her progress in breaking down male domination in the world, she fails to perceive that she is as firmly hooked as ever on his orgasmic sexuality and his clitoral substitute for love. Her protests are really about love, not equality; but that's not heard in the strident male arena. It is man's world and he built it on the strength of sexual aggression. Male domination began in sex and in sex it continues unabated. Woman cannot alter this position by marching with banners or withdrawing from sex. She has tried all the means at her disposal down through the centuries; none has worked and none will. The solution is now beyond the scope of any personal or social action. Only consciousness beyond the person or divine action can help.

Let me ask you woman, have you really any idea how to free yourself from male sexual domination? How to bring real love back into your life? Any idea how you and your partner can learn to make real love? To truly make love tangible so that you can actually create love together and build on it as long as you are both together? Have you?

If you have an answer, please say it. Say it now out loud or to someone else — before I tell you. Or before you're tempted, after I tell you, to say you knew it all along.

Well, whatever your answer, I ask you to give it up. To find love you have to abandon all your preconceptions. The only way to love is to be available to the new, now.

Addressing both man and woman, if you are going to bring love into your sexual life, you are going to need new energy. That energy starts with honesty — honesty to yourself and honesty to life.

Here are three things you can do to gather the necessary energy.

Listen to yourself admit that your love-life is not good enough. You must express this. Say it aloud. Hear it so that there is no hiding, no psychological escaping. It's not enough just to know it inside. That's how love dies between lovers. They think it's enough to know they love inside and not to say it any more. When it's too late they sob and scream their love; but the door's already slammed, the house empty. Say it now so that your whole being hears it: 'Our lovemaking is not good enough.'

Next, admit to yourself that you don't know what to do about the problem; that you are powerless. See that all you can do is repeat the same old actions that men and women in their desperation and despair have taken unsuccessfully since they first fell in love and time or emotion started to come between them. Be honest. If you already know the answers, why haven't you acted on them? And if you have the answer, why are you reading this book?

Finally, admit you can't do it alone, that you need help. For when you give up, when you truly surrender in humility, help is always there within you. And then it can appear outside you.

Such honesty and self-knowledge generates passion — the power of love and true commitment in existence. The word passion originally meant suffering — not the suffering of love but the suffering of self. It's the dissolution or death of self that gives rise to true passion.

Self consists of all your past emotional and mental suffering that persists to this day in your subconscious. And the most potent component of self is sexual unhappiness — all the heartbreak, sexual frustration, and discontent that you've suffered since your earliest sexual experience. In other words self is the ignorance in love and the pain that that causes.

Like everything else in existence, self naturally does not want to die. It is sustained by love of self instead of love of love. However the time comes for everybody when self *must* die, like everything. This is the moment for love to come deeper into the body. And as self is dissolved (it is always a painful, traumatic process) true passion is present, as it was in the beginning.

To return to the golden state of love in these confused and ignorant times is not easy. But if you have the courage, the honesty, and really desire your freedom, your love, I will guide you into living it.

A LESSON IN LOVE

I've spoken about how far man and woman are today from the divine and golden love that is their birthright. Now we are ready to start reclaiming it. I'm going to take you through a number of steps, a programme of lessons in lovemaking if you care to call it that, and I ask you to please follow it carefully, putting what is said into practice in your own time over the months and years ahead. This is a process. Every step is the means, not the end. The instruction in this book leads you closer and closer to the reality of love; but you can't make it happen quickly or with any will of your own. Love has to be allowed to work in you, as love will. In the beginning and for a good while thereafter, you have much to unlearn, and many habits to dismantle.

To begin with there are four requirements: commitment, absence of emotion, practice and perseverance.

Both partners must be committed.

To make love in this new way both you and your partner must be committed to take the necessary steps. Both of you should read this book, and preferably read it out loud together, at least in the beginning. Don't think that reading it once or twice is enough. Both of you must be willing to follow the instructions. Adapt them sensibly to your own particular situation, when you see the necessity.

Do not give up, no matter how hard things get or how often you seem to fail. Keep a sense of greater purpose. You are both engaged in the restoration of divine love on this planet, whatever that may mean to you personally at this time.

If you are reading this but do not have a partner now, it is a preparation for when you do. For you this is an exercise in seeing the errors you've made in the past.

Make love without emotion or imagination.

You are going to practise making love without emotion or imagination. The purpose of this is for you to learn to leave it to the two bodies — to get your habitual controlling self out of the action.

You may not get the idea at the first attempt. Or you might.

At first, the lovemaking may seem strange, even cold.

Make love frequently.

Make love as often as you can. For only by making love, or endeavouring to, can you make love. The less you make love, the more you grow apart. Don't allow too long a gap.

I repeat: make love. Don't make excuses. Put the bodies together and see.

Please persevere.

There'll be a setback sooner or later as emotion or self comes in. But don't be discouraged. Keep going. Keep loving.

If the emotion in either or both of you is too great to allow straightness or love, break off and try again next day. The connection will return. Or it will come suddenly and then fade out again as you go through another wave of emotion that separates you.

Some of these emotional periods may last several days. During them you may even dislike each other. Lovemaking can seem impossible. Try when you can, though.

You can't rid yourself of all the past at once. Or even in a few weeks. You actually have to work at it for the rest of your life. All the time you will be making more love, becoming a more loving and conscious man or woman.

Next I'm going to say several things about how to be together in straightness and love.

Do not be independent.

In the lead-up to lovemaking and in the lovemaking act itself, have no thoughts or decisions independent of your partner. Everything is to be done together and discussed and observed together — as you do it.

No long silences.

Converse constantly, expressing in words what you are feeling as a bodily sensation. When you feel plea- sure, say it. Say 'That's lovely'; if it is. Say what you actually feel, not what you think. You are not sup- posed to be thinking. You are supposed to be being. That means looking inside your body at the sensation, not at what you are thinking. Communicating in words will keep you conscious and present, in front of each other.

No promiscuity.

Don't spread yourselves around sexually. Conserve the energy of this practice. It is precious. Committed partners are not easy to find. Keep to the one partner, once you've found him or her. Partners who are not committed will weaken you and make you lose faith.

If you are without a partner, my advice is to wait. Don't go with someone for emotional gratification or sexual satisfaction. Wait until someone comes who has enough love to be with you in the ways I'm revealing. If you meet someone and you enjoy being with each other, be straight right from the start. Tell him or her the truth; that you are endeavouring to love and raise your consciousness through love and honesty — honest love. Take responsibility. Talk about what it involves. And if you are serious and earnest about loving, you will eventually draw to yourself a person who will share the start of this great adventure with you.

If the partnership ends after a while, nothing is really lost. Both of you have gained in love and consciousness and can be that much more loving and straight next time.

Be vulnerable to love.

This is most important, especially for woman. Don't cut yourself off because you've been hurt in the past. Be brave for love. Turn outward. Love will help you. Don't let fear harden you. The hurt was emotion and lack of love, in both of you. It's past. Let it go. Now that you're beginning to understand what making love is about, you have the simple answer to the hurt and the simplest protection against it: that is, only make love where there is enough love to be straight and to be present with each other.

Don't fall in love. Be in love.

Falling in love is closing your eyes, shutting down your beautiful consciousness and tripping off into dreamland while you're awake. It's bound to end in disaster because you'll be in imagination; you won't see what's going on. But *be* in love. Always be in love when you are in love. For to be in love and to keep love fresh and new requires tremendous awareness, tremendous presence.

Be in love in this way and your love will not end, for love has no end. Fall in love and your love will end.

For both of you the conscious purpose is to reduce the emotionality in yourselves. And the next step is to watch for the moment when the emotion enters and see why you allow it. I'm going to mention five areas of emotionality that may undermine your ability to make love. These are: doubt, disinclination, over-excitability, defensiveness and argument.

Agree about when and where you will make love.

You should decide together in advance when you are going to make love. Allow ample time. No rush. No avoidable distractions.

It is imperative that the woman sticks to her decision to make love. If there has to be a timelag due to work or children, she must make it clear to the man that when the time comes she won't have a headache, or not feel like it, or be too tired. She must take responsibility for herself, as he must for himself. Her declared position must be, 'I am going to make love with you. There's no reason to be impatient or doubtful. I won't change my mind'.

Otherwise, as the time approaches he will start getting anxious, excited and impatient. He can't help this when there is any possibility of lovemaking. His subconscious fear is that she will change her mind — that for some reason he won't get there. Excitement comes from anticipating an end, in this case an orgasm, and he has yet to learn that making love is not an end, not an orgasm; that when he can make love and go on and on, his woman will be available all the time and at any time.

Who's not available for love? Only those who don't know love.

So the woman has to consciously dispel the man's mounting excitement by reaffirming her availability. Woman's implied unavailability excites man and makes him a hopeless lover because then he wants her instead of loving her; and wanting soon runs out or tires, as every woman who has ever excited a man knows.

On the other hand, if your physical relationship is old and weary, the problem won't be excitement, but how to be new, fresh and present every moment as you face each other.

Making love as I am describing it will give you both a new approach, a new energetic interest to find out if it works. That will help to keep the old habitual self out; and allow the present in.

'But I don't feel like it.' No more of that! You don't have to worry about 'feeling like making love'. That's an emotional distraction. The bodies love to make love. The part of you that feels like it or doesn't feel like it is the problem, the emotional monitor, the self that gets in the way. Leave it to the bodies and they will make love. Stay out of it as much as you can.

Keep the sexual temperature down.

Due to woman's innate lack of sexual excitability, she is likely to be stronger or straighter than the man and is more likely to grasp the spirit of what I'm endeavouring to convey. She must keep the man straight by seeing that he does not lapse into his imagination. For without him realising it, his mind will start to throw up erotic and sexual pictures or thoughts that have nothing to do with the woman he's with. She must constantly work at keeping his sexual temperature down. He might well say, 'But this is like visiting the doctor!' Make a joke if you like. And smile. Making love like this may indeed feel as clinical as a visit to the doctor. That's how it's supposed to be, until you break through your past habits.

Stay clear of the emotion.

The woman can quite suddenly get off balance, particularly if she is near her menstrual period, when she is often acutely defensive and suspicious of man as well as herself. This suspicion is global and reflects man's age-old exploitation of her through her children, the young she must protect.

Also, her female perception is heightened at this time and is in conflict with the male emotionality in her, which tries to project itself out into man's world. She can become confused and unsure of her role, so he must keep her straight too. He must be alert to see that she stays present.

Do not accuse each other.

You must not accuse each other of being emotional as this will only generate more emotion. If one of you suspects that the partner is emotional or not being straight, you must ask a question. For example, 'What are you feeling now?' or 'Is it true now?' Always refer to now, not to yesterday. If each of you answers honestly and you stay present (as you are committed to do) you will see yourself being emotional, if you are. Then if you admit it without argument or justification, the emotion will be dispelled and love will remain. Keep talking, but always to the point — what both of you are doing and feeling now. Trust each other. Listen to each other.

Do not dream off. Keep each other present. Don't be upset when your partner says you're not present. Resist the urge to argue back. There is nothing to defend if you are straight, honest. Discover together. Hear each other. You'll soon get the hang of it.

Now to the preliminaries of lovemaking. Remember that the purpose is to consciously reduce your excitability. Therefore you have to abandon your habitual foreplay, which you've been accustomed to using to get yourselves excited.

The time has come.

You have agreed to make love and now it's time. Undress in the same room. Keep the light on. No hiding. Don't be concentrated. Love is a serious business but it's not that serious. Be easy. You can smile. Just raise the corners of the lips and smile. Be present. Be in the room there together, be now. Stand naked and apart. Look at each other, eyes and body. See each other's bodies. No judging, no thinking. Don't think about what's going to happen or what you're going to do.

Please don't be self-conscious. Hold to love. Start by accepting your body, being your body, blemishes and all. If you see that your partner is self-conscious, help him, help her. Smile. See something good. Look for the beauty of the being within, coming through the body. It's there. See it. Say it. Be naked psychologically. Be innocent. Be new. Don't look back. Be yourself just as you are, now. Be vulnerable. You've got nothing to lose that wasn't lost a long, long time ago.

While you are looking at each other, do so without using the imagination. Do not jump from this moment into the next move. If you think or use the imagination it's likely to project you, when the time comes, into making love to someone else, with a vagina or penis that's not really there.

Have you lost the urge to make love? Not really. The body doesn't lose the urge to make love. It will always enjoy making love if you — the monitor — don't get in the way.

Lie down and embrace. This is when the imagination is likely to become active — if you're looking over your partner's shoulder or when you close your eyes. So don't close your eyes. Feel your partner's flesh, on the back and the arms. Don't think. Feel. And keep the eyes open.

He gives to her.

He caresses and fondles her. She caresses and holds him — in love. But at this stage she must not fondle his genitals. She remains passive, responsive but undemonstrative. His job is to please and delight her — to give to her without exciting himself. He focuses only on pleasing her. That will give him pleasure — without emotion. This is the most important point for him to remember. He is not to take for himself. He is to give — and then give again. And again.

Kissing.

When you kiss, kiss gently and lightly on the lips and the body. But do not use your tongue. Lovers lose and hide themselves in tongue-kissing. The tongue can be used like an emotional penis. Love is made consciously in the vagina and you are not there yet. There must be no surrogate for the love of the penis in the vagina. Later, when you have learnt to be fully present there, you can do anything your mutual passion requires.

Feel your love in your solar plexus.

Put your attention on the solar plexus, for that's where passion starts — before it spills over into the genitals. The woman will probably be able to feel the solar plexus before the man does. In his excitement he is likely to miss it and connect up with the emotion in his penis.

Stay with your love. Keep yourself and your partner present by saying what you are feeling — out loud. If you feel passion rising, or excitation, or excitement, say it.

The man may lose his erection.

The man may not have an erection; or if he does he may lose it. He may have become so dependent on imagination that he can't get an erection without it. This is likely if his lovemaking has been habitual in the past. If he gets an erection and then loses it because the stimulus of the imagination is missing, that has to be seen as a good thing; because he is less likely to ejaculate prematurely when he eventually becomes erect inside her.

An erection is only necessary in the vagina, where love is made. So he doesn't need an erection at this stage. He doesn't require an erection to feel passionate and loving, or to inhale the spiritual fragrance of her feminine presence. He may kiss her breasts and fondle her genitals (without finger penetration) to show his love to her, through his hands. As he loves her like this her passion will be rising.

If he has a full, hard erection outside the vagina he is already in danger of being emotional. This is normal today and he should not feel disheartened. He's just got to try to keep the imagined stimulus out and has to be very aware and still as he enters her, or he may ejaculate prematurely. A penis erected outside the vagina usually has an emotional will of its own, which is really the force of wanting. Inside the vagina a man can use that force to suppress his climax. But as suppression is not love, the lovemaking will not be satisfactory to either him or her. Eventually ejaculation is mastered by speed of consciousness or presence which comes from absence of self-consideration.

Before he enters her, they enjoy each other and at the same time consciously contain their excitement. He is alert to see that she is really present, especially if she is enjoying his caress. She speaks to him, reminding him to keep his sexual excitement in check and helps him to interrupt and so break up the force of his wanting. They keep talking, always to the point of what each is feeling now. No long silences, remember. No blissful spells of euphoria. If the sensation is sweet, beautiful, nice, lovely (whatever the right word is) she says so. His job is to love her by pleasing her and she responds and acknowledges his loving.

She does not observe her feelings, her emotions. She aims to *be* the sensation in her body. She gets her consciousness into the part of the body where the pleasure actually is.

The aim is to contain your excitement, so foreplay is minimal. Often there will be no foreplay at all. Foreplay is like forethought; there's a sense of premeditated intent. You work towards the exciting prospect of the pleasure to come. Or you repeat pleasurable feelings out of the past in yourself. The present, or love without intention, is ignored. When you both know that you're able to stay with the pleasure without getting excited you'll be able to engage in loveplay. I'll say more about that later, but first you must practise making love without excitement.

※

So, bring your bodies together and make love. Remember: hold the imagination at bay. Don't drift into thought. Your aim is to be conscious of the pleasure throughout. As you come together please be emotionally detached. That means you are present in love but detached from the memory, the past. You are aware, patient, considerate, giving, and able to see the funny side should that occur to you.

He enters her gently and lovingly.

Gentle firmness is the way of love. Nothing must be forced. If necessary, use a lubricant. He must enter her slowly. As he enters, he is one with the sensation in his penis. This means he must feel what his penis is feeling every moment — not just the urgency, the pressure of his own wanting. He must get to know the difference.

If he doesn't have a full erection he may be helped into the vagina. She avoids fondling his penis to stimulate him. If there's sufficient love between them, he will have enough of an erection to enter. Or he will lie against her until the love comes through. It can't be hurried or forced. Once inside, the penis will become fuller or fully erect. The man sees for himself that given presence and love in both partners, the penis always responds in the vagina — without need of stimulation beforehand. It's the same when the man is apparently impotent. Put the soft penis into the vagina. Wait patiently. Or get up and try later or the next day.

You are switching over to love as the guiding power and you must have faith in it. As soon as there is com-munication and the love flows, the penis will suddenly move like a living thing and extend towards the vagina. This will amaze you both (particularly the man) and you will begin to understand the wonderful power and intelligence you're connecting with.

On entry the man must be prepared for a downrush of her sexual energy. This will make him come with the penis only partly erect; and this may astonish or puzzle him. But the more she learns to stay present and to be united with the consciousness or pleasure in her vagina, the less the release of this energy will hinder him.

All thought must be kept out.

Once inside, he penetrates as far as he can and then lies still. He allows his penis to feel her, to absorb the vaginal energy. That will inform the penis of what to do, what is needed. He responds only to his penis, not to what he has learned, heard or can remember. He keeps the past out of it — all past experience as thought. He is as new as the moment itself. Then the penis can do its divine work.

There are no practised moves.

She makes no deliberate movements with her body. All movement is left for the body to do, even if it means no movement at all. She does nothing that she's learned from other lovers, or acquired through reading or watching films. In the beginning it may not be easy for the woman to distinguish between body contortions, contriving phony signs of pleasure and participation, and pure, natural movements made under the control of the vaginal consciousness. Later, the body will move passionately (but not necessarily demonstratively) according to the consciousness of the moment. But to start with, all extremes of movement in her are suspect. In particular, she must abandon any 'male' assertiveness or aggression. She must remember that love in woman is not projective. It is a still, sweet, natural, flowing motion. Flexing the muscles of the vagina is a good trick and is sure to entertain an emotional penis, but it is not love.

There is no imagination in the penis.

The man does not allow his mind to move. He gets his consciousness out of his head and down into his penis where the love is being made. He stays present, without imagining where the penis is. His penis has no imagination — only the knowledge of what is, where it is. He must be that sensation, that highly sensitive consciousness which responds in perfect harmony to the energetic needs of the vaginal consciousness.

Continue to keep up the loving dialogue, telling each other how beautiful it is and how much you love making love — if that is the truth.

Ejaculation is not inevitable.

One thought about where his penis is and he is more likely to ejaculate; but the moment he feels he can't stop himself is the moment he can. He must not believe the first feeling that orgasm is inevitable. He must not give in to it. It is a trick of the pent-up emotion that wants to be released, part of the animal drive to masturbate or reproduce. When the feeling comes, he must cease all movement, be completely still, or withdraw immediately. He will discover which is best for him. The split second is crucial. It marks the point where he can use his creative spiritual authority, or presence as man, and resist or dispel the instinctive animal emotion. He must not go with the inevitability, must not believe he can't stop, because he can. Only in the *next* instant is orgasm inevitable. Not *now*.

Please do not misunderstand. The man is not continuously trying to avoid coming. His consciousness is on the action of love, not the possible end result. Orgasm is not to be seen as good or bad, necessary or unnecessary, desirable or undesirable. The orgasm comes when it comes, naturally. The point is that the man must learn to exercise his authority or presence over the excitability or past in him. His ejaculation must not be a problem for either him or her.

The penis opens the vagina.

He endeavours to stay near the top of the vagina. He's not in a hurry to move backwards and forwards, up and down. The vagina is an elastic cavity, taut with hidden tension, and the head of the penis should open it up, absorbing the stress and residual emotion out of the whole upper and lower area. He should move from one wall of the vagina to the other several times, pausing for a few seconds between each movement. The proper function of the penis in the first instance is to remove the woman's tensions from the vagina, where they reside. The penis can start to do this as the woman learns to reduce in her daily life the projection of her inner tensions as personality, needless activity or emotionality.

When the man becomes sexually still and present, the head of the penis acts like a highly charged magnet. First it gathers the vaginal tensions. Then it begins to collect the divine energies. The purpose of the lovemaking is served when the divine energies have been gathered.

He may then lose his erection inside the vagina without having an orgasm.

After making love consistently in this new way, and as you persevere with it, you will be able to make love for lengthening periods, to your mutual love and delight. Her vagina will become softer, more sensitive and receptive, and will no longer necessarily need external stimulation. Only emotional tension makes the vagina resistant or not ready for love. As the emotional tension is reduced, the consciousness or sensitivity of the vagina increases, and her joy in lovemaking grows. And as he becomes less dependent on excitement he grows in presence and a new sense of command and authority appears in his life.

Remember: only what he can take, can she give. And she must learn to take more and more pleasure from his lovemaking without herself becoming excited. Eventually, maximum pleasure prolonged in lovemaking transforms into beauty. Making love is beautiful, and everyone loves it as the vagina and penis become honest and free.

THE PROBLEM OF SEX

*T*n this section I will be going further into the causes of sexual unhappiness, how to deal with sexual problems and how to get your lovemaking right, which means making love without emotion.

In love without emotion, there are no love problems. What is emotion? What am I talking about? Let's get it straight. Emotion is the living substance of the past, what you believed in and what you were in the past. It's your self. It lives on in your subconscious. It's not you now, the intelligence reading this now, in the present. But it's there now, just under the surface of your awareness. And it will rise and take over your relaxed intelligence the instant you are reminded of someone or something in the past which disturbed you or caused you pain.

Let me demonstrate. While reading this book now,

suppose you are reminded that you're unhappy in your relationship with a partner or lover. That emotion is the past; relating to the way he or she hasn't loved you enough in the past or how they spoke to you or misunderstood you even a minute ago. (A minute or a second ago is the past.) So your intelligence gets distracted from the present pleasant act of reading and relates or reflects on the past; and you feel unhappy in your self. It's your self, the past, that is unhappy, not the intelligence in the present.

Whenever you are resentful, depressed, angry, or jealous you are feeling the emotional substance of your self in the past. And because your intelligence identifies with it you become your past self and repeat the behaviour of all those old emotions, often much to your intelligent distress. You even wonder where the emotion comes from — arising so instantaneously, too. Well, that's your past hurt self, reacting as pain to the present. So you lose the present which is actually your presence. In short, you lose your presence.

Your emotional self is always trying to come back and live on in you, to take you over and use you as it always has done. When your words or feelings come from the past, from the recall of any hurtful moment before now, you are being emotional. You are not straight, not yourself. So you can't be love or make love to your full potential.

All this means that you can only make love in the present, when you haven't lost your presence. So the first step is to learn how to leave your self behind and not allow it to enter and spoil the lovemaking. Much easier said than done. And here's the reason why. The substance of every past sexual emotion you've ever had — both the excitation and the pain — has accumulated in your genitals and lodged there, or in that part of the brain that controls them. It gathers there as unsuspected tension, as the desire to repeat pleasurable experiences and to avoid repeating hurtful ones. In women, the tension manifests physically as a subtle tightness in the vagina and sometimes as an acute tightness. Psychologically it produces involuntary thoughts and emotions associated with past sexual pleasure. This may drive the woman to masturbate. The self-ish emotional pleasure of masturbation, in which there is no love or man to contend with, joins the vaginal tension as the desire to repeat itself and so the habit is perpetuated.

In man the effect of all his past unresolved sexual emotions — the pleasurable and the painful — is a hardening of the penis in the act of making love. The penis when erect should be firm but not hard. Since a hard penis is likely to draw to itself a similarly hard or tense vagina, the woman may not be able to tell the difference. Such a woman may be so attuned to sexual excitement that a firm and loving penis can hardly be felt. Or the loving penis may be so out of synchronisation with the excitable vagina that either it refuses to erect or will repeatedly withdraw, refusing to remain inside. The hardening sexual tension in man also expresses itself as involuntary erections. In both sexes, this genital tension causes restlessness, heaviness and discontent.

Every vagina, until loved rightly, is an emotional vagina, relatively stiff, muscley, expectant, self-guarding and narrowly receptive. Though the actual vaginal tension may be imperceptible to the woman she will feel the effects in the play of her emotions. A vagina used by many emotional men starts to react like the emotional penis itself. It becomes hard, greedy and predatory, and concentrates on orgasm. When a vagina is sexually hungry like this, very little awareness of love is generated in the woman herself. She feels love within like any other woman but when intercourse begins the love is swamped by the pleasure of the excitement or the drive for orgasm. The pleasure, being based on temporary emotional satisfaction, produces deep inner unhappiness. She may have been promiscuous (it was only her desperate search for love) or she may have had only one previous lover, but still her vagina will respond to whatever energy man has put into it.

The purifying process in the vagina starts through contact with a penis that has not surrendered to the selfish drive of sex, but has served love and developed sufficiently in consciousness. The vagina freed of emotion becomes yielding, soft, giving, simple, easy, undemanding and still. Then, to the woman, the love-making is sweeter and more fulfilling. It is effortless, natural and beautiful — with the emphasis on beauty, since beauty is the divine culmination of the simple pleasure of making love.

The vagina is essentially passive and innocent, the organ of love. It learns all its bad habits from the male. The penis is the guru or teacher of the vagina, for better or for worse.

At birth the female psyche is love innocent — open during a girl's early years and absorbing every influence of love and sex in the family and the wider world. And with so much past in the species, the vagina is potentially emotional from infancy. Every girl, as she grows up, psychically absorbs some of the sexuality and sexual frustration of her father, brothers, other male relatives, boyfriends and the male-dominated media and society around her. Later, after puberty, the vagina's emotional potential is actualised and every girl falls into the normal and predictable problems of love.

Love nourishes her psyche. But the projected sexual influences lay a patina of mental excitation over the love. At a very early age this causes her to fall into romantic sexual imaginings and daydreaming, the recip-rocal of which is fear. Even before the penis touches her, the virgin vagina is tense with emotional fantasies, excitement and immature sexual experience, such as petting, masturbation and fingering by boys. As soon as she comes into contact with male sexuality she is contaminated by the seed of discontent and immediately disillusioned by man's lack of love. The first time she is penetrated the pain may keep her momentarily in the present, but she will soon dream off into the past, into emotion and fantasy.

It is ignorance of love in the world that maintains this basic tension in all girls and in every virgin vagina. Once, when time and the human race were very young, every virgin girl understood love, because she was love. There was no ignorance of love in her consciousness as there was no emotion in her vagina. Her lack of physical experience did not cause tension because she understood love before she made it. Now the virgin no longer understands love or herself. There are no real teachers, gurus, able to instruct her before wrong impressions are formed in her by unhappy sexual experiences; and no society loving enough to permit this fundamental education.

With no understanding of love, the virgin imagines what physical love is. And that generates the tension, the vaginal emotion, even hysteria. As the years go by, and her experience grows, the tension accumulates. Most women's experience of lovemaking contains repeated disappointment. Most men's experience consists of automatic excitement at the prospect of ejaculation. Between woman's fears, reservations and hopes, all based on past experience, and his dancing excitement, also based on past experience, there is very little chance of real love being made between them in the present, the here and now. So more emotion than love will be produced.

By trying to repeat a good sexual experience like coming, you make yourself expectant or emotional. And by trying to avoid the repetition of a bad experience, you make yourself emotionally wary and cautious. In neither condition can you make love.

The alarming truth which is not realised is that the emotion produced in what was supposed to be love-making will surface within a few minutes, hours or days, and cause a bout of depression or discontent, particularly in woman. In man, the emotion will surface as irritability, anger or aggressive behaviour and he probably will release it further with masturbation.

The penis is only really happy when erected inside the vaginal profundity of woman. Erected in the emptiness of space outside the vagina, the penis is impatient, excitable and emotional. In this unnatural state it is naturally regarded by society as obscene, and often as threatening. This is because the penis erected outside its natural vaginal home is a projection of sexual aggression. For all men such an erection is demanding and discomfiting; frequently he will have to masturbate to release the pressure of its misplaced, lonely existence.

We are all sexually loaded, ready to go off emotionally as soon as intercourse is a possibility. Sexual emotion is there inside you now. It is waiting to take a man over and erupt as premature ejaculation or sexual selfishness at the first opportunity. Especially if he is a man who studies pornographic magazines and videos or suggestive pictures. It is waiting to take over every woman with a bad sexual experience, for every broken love affair is still inside her.

It is not possible to name or know all past experiences associated with sexual emotion, stretching back to childhood. They have coalesced into one deep, dark complex that is far too complicated and obscure to ever be defined. So how do you rid yourself of it, so that you can begin to love rightly? What can you do? Where do you start?

You remove the emotion from yourselves in the approach to lovemaking. You make love without excitement, expectation or imagination. You have to be very present, very aware, and conscious of everything you do as you come together.

∽

I suggest you engage in only minimal foreplay, or even none at all, because that will help you to realise as a new conscious experience that only the penis and vagina together make love, nothing else. All else is imagination and an avoidance of the responsibility of love now. This is the simple truth that man and woman have forgotten. They show they've forgotten it by continuously getting carried away with imaginative substitutes for love.

No matter how many delightful love stories you read or hear, how many erotic movies you see, or what sex games you engage in, the magic and romance between you and your lover still fades — because all those substitutes for love dull the perception and prevent you from staying with and facing the simple truth, the reality of love now. It is the imagination that takes you out of now. The imagination that man developed in building his world. On the wings of imagination he takes off and leaves his body, the earth, his love and woman. And as she is also addicted to imagination, she flies off after him.

Foreplay feeds the imagination and prevents you from being with the reality of love now. If you can see the truth of what I am saying it will be a mighty moment in your life.

For a man or woman who are being themselves all the normal social flirtations and passionate petting before lovemaking are a way of avoiding direct responsibility for love now. Sex-games are like a stiff whisky, a dose of the wrong spirit to try to get our courage up or a drug to help us forget what we're doing because we're not prepared yet to face up to the reality that love is made now, not in some imagined future. So, as is usual in the man-made world, the truth is the reverse of what's accepted and practised. The world plays games and doesn't make love. The truth is: make love and you don't need to play games.

There is no love in imagination. Why do you need the imagination anyway? To get in the mood? To get an erection? Nonsense. You just think you need it because of a habit most of the world has got into through lack of love and understanding. It's a very difficult habit to break, but you've got to do it. You don't need your imagination to make love because you are with the real thing. The actual living man or woman gives you the most delicious, pleasurable sensation that you can have — in the flesh and not the mind.

The people of the earth have been hoaxed by the imagination. Down through the ages, children and adults have been masturbating and making love in the imagination, unaware that the imagery is utter self-delusion and a cruel addiction. Because everyone indulges in the same drug, its loveless escapism is considered normal and even necessary without being considered at all.

Let me anticipate a question that will arise in many men. How do you masturbate without imagination?

You, the adult, can't. When you cease imagining and fantasising about love, the masturbation stops. The imagination is the habit, not the masturbation. The imagination stirs the sexual emotionality like a whirlpool and that momentum drives you to masturbate.

If you have to masturbate (and the pressure to do so is intense, particularly in the male) use as few images as you can. Don't use faces. No one ever made love to a face except in their imagination. If you are a man, use only the image of the female genitals. Get the images down to that alone, because that is closest to the actuality.

Wean yourself from the habit by not thinking or lusting after the opposite sex and the impulse to masturbate will gradually disappear. You can get yourself off the global drug of sexual imagination. Start now. Be in your senses. Be out of your mind — and in your body. Be where you are. Be responsible.

But if you do masturbate don't feel guilty and don't allow your children to feel guilty, if they confide in you. Guilt distorts the personality in both the young and the adult. The error is not in the act of masturbating. It's in the misuse of the imagination, not only during the act but more importantly during the rest of the normal daily activities when the mind is allowed to roam wherever it pleases.

The compulsion to masturbate is almost universal today. It arose in the evolutionary past from the instinctive male drive in all animal species to mate and reproduce. In the case of the human animal the addition of self-consciousness allowed reflection on its own organism, behaviour, emotional reactions and memory. This faculty was denied the rest of the species but it has its downside. In man and woman it produces guilt and self-doubt.

The male monkey in the zoo masturbates with outrageous detachment and lack of guilt. Unlike man he couldn't care less. That's because he can't see himself, can't imagine. The monkey only feels. But he can't feel he feels, can't know it. So the monkey can't make love. The power to make love, which man alone possesses, is the self-reflection that distinguishes him from the rest of the animal species. However, when he misuses this unique creative gift by reflecting on past sexual images and past emotions, he taps back into his animal past, into the mechanical animal drive, and masturbates or mates without love. He is then unhappy.

If the monkey had the creative power to make love he would see himself masturbating and feel wretched too. But his only option is to masturbate or reproduce. I've only seen monkeys masturbate in captivity, not in the wild. Since man is the captive of his mind, and not yet the master of his imagination, he masturbates.

Now, the question of impotence. Impotence is not necessarily a sign of physical deterioration or masculine deficiency. Healthy young men suffer from it. Nor is the cause psychological — due to fear — as some therapists may claim. Fear is not the cause. Fear is an effect.

Where there is no physical impairment through ill-health, disease or damage to the penis, the cause of impotence is selfishness. Impotence arises from the unwillingness to truly love woman physically unless there's something in it for yourself; unless you feel like it or think it's your duty. All of these reasons are excuses for not being able to love. Whether you feel like it, or don't feel like it, is irrelevant. In love you love simply for the beauty of loving woman.

Impotence has become an excusable condition of our times, particularly in busy men and older men. It's an acceptable feature of man's stressful unhappy life today, catered for by a medical profession that suffers the same stress and unhappiness. The whole male society is in the same condition of selfishness; so no one offers the true diagnosis or real cure and all are excused for failing to take responsibility for love.

Impotence is caused by lack of love. However, since an erection may be induced through excitement, failure to erect can also be due to lack of emotionality. When men get older they're more likely to have difficulty getting an erection because living has knocked some of the emotional excitement out of them. And by then, in love-making there's so often not enough love in their bodies or the woman's.

The penis will not become erect without either sexual emotion or love. Often when couples become physically bored with each other and have intercourse out of a sense of duty, there is neither the emotional drive nor enough love or consciousness between them. So the man will not be able to get an erection. If the man has emotional drive but no love, he will have no trouble. He will induce his erection by emotionality or sexual aggression. An emotional penis becomes erect to gratify itself and doesn't need love to have sex, as every woman knows. So it will probably be a one-sided affair although if the woman can get herself into the same condition (which she can do, due to her induced male-ness) the couple can gratify each other — but it won't be love.

When a penis is responsive to love and not emotion it becomes fully erect only inside the vagina or just before entering it. A loving vagina has no difficulty admitting a loosely-full loving penis which then imme-diately becomes firm, authoritative and erect for the purpose of love.

However if the woman starts dreaming off, or is sexually demanding, there may not be enough love in her vagina to sustain the erection, especially if the man is endeavouring to purify himself. This man does not use the imagination but finds sufficient stimulus in the moment and the woman he is with. He does not become disturbed by a temporary loss of erection. He is patient and waits, available for the moment when love returns.

The main physical problem in lovemaking is man's premature ejaculation. And woman unsuspectingly contributes to it.

The man who comes prematurely has temporarily lost the will to love, has lost himself, therefore cannot take the complete surrender of woman and is without real authority. He knows it and is shamed by it. The only valid authority man can have over woman is through love; and that authority she will concede to him unconditionally when he demonstrates sufficient love to accept and take her total surrender. Only what he can take, can she give. His trumped-up economic and physical authority over her during the last few thousand years has been a nasty bit of work — getting even with her for his own weakness, the abdication of his true authority.

As selfless and munificent as a truly loving woman

can be, the tragic division between her and her lover goes on from generation to generation, because man has forgotten himself, forgotten how to love; and woman cannot give herself, cannot reach her natural fulfilment without him.

Premature ejaculation is caused by excitement and anticipation in both the man and the woman. This is there before any foreplay and long before the physical act begins. In man there is continuous, pre-sexual excitation, a heightened aggression, due to normal sexual fantasising. He keeps the basic level of aggression relatively high through his obsession with sex — thinking about sex, reading about sex, joking and talking about it with other men, slyly alluding to it in mixed company; looking at women in public, consciously lusting after them, and making habitually unconscious sexual connections with them. He continually maintains and excites the sexual emotion. So his sexual thermometer is normally registering (let's say) twenty-five degrees of emotion.

By contrast, woman is normally only at say five degrees. Woman is basically less aggressive than man because she is not basically obsessed with sex. Because man is sex-obsessed, he is ready for sex at any time, unless his numerous hang-ups and inhibitions get in the way. Woman is not; unless she is truly in love. For her to want to make love, her normal sexual temperature has to be raised.

In the foreplay before intercourse, flirting, touching, kissing and the fondling of breasts and genitals raises the sexual temperature of both parties. When this excitement is added to the normally raised level of stimulation in the man, it makes him fantasise much more than her. So his sexual temperature rises at a faster rate. By the time he's close to entering her, he is at a burning ninety-nine degrees and rising rapidly with expectation and impatience. She is at a comfortable and enjoyable seventy degrees and rising too. Sometimes she has only to open her legs to him, his fantasy-image realised, and he ejaculates. Or his penis merely touches her. Or just penetrates the lips of the vagina. Or he might actually manage to get inside the vagina before he comes. In seconds his sexual temperature drops from a feverish one hundred plus degrees, to nil, as he selfishly ejaculates himself back to the rare state of cool, selfless absence of wanting.

Woman's contribution to the premature ejaculation of the man is subtle and you'll have to examine what I'm going to say closely in your own experience to grasp or test the truth of it. It's not something that all women experience, so if it's not the truth for you don't imagine or invent it for yourself.

In the young vagina, the insufficiently loved vagina and the excitable vagina, there is a particular response to the penetration of the penis — a downrush of energy from the upper body, a spasm of repressed love. As a surge of love, it's meant to draw the penis up into the highest part of the vagina towards the womb. But even the practised lover may feel it as a sudden, intense wave, and the shock or force of it draws the sexual emotion out of him, and he ejaculates. As the woman learns to release her love gently and smoothly in the vagina, the pressure on her partner to orgasm is eased. And as he in turn practises reducing his sexual excitement, the problem of premature ejaculation diminishes.

As far as man is concerned ejaculation usually marks the end of the act. But even if he has brought her to orgasm, a selfish lover will still not have collected her finer energies. Her orgasm will have released or dispersed her immediate sexual emotion. But the higher divine energies that remain uncollected will eventually degenerate into emotional demand and discontent. All emotion in woman is the demand or the cry to be truly loved — not used as a sexual spittoon.

But woman, thank God, is love. Love is her true nature underneath all the emotion, notions and hang-ups. If she loves him, or if she just loves, she can bear the sexual disappointment. Woman at every level represents the mother — the true archetypal female, Mother Earth, in which all of us delight and find our pleasure (even if only via the whisky made of earth's grain and water).

Man is like a child to the boundless love in true woman, which every woman, underneath her unhappiness, knows herself to be. In her love, she can forgive him for coming and nullify her own desire. She can absorb the restless energy of his orgasm, holding him there inside her, boyish and new in his brief moment of peace.

For woman, the fulfilment of her love is to take him into her, to take everything he can give, and everything he is, while in return offering up every bit of herself in sweet, complete surrender to love. When he comes prematurely he is not mature enough to give her all of himself. He hasn't got the time. So she in turn is unable to give him all the love she has to give. By coming, he goes. He leaves her. Because of it, he is a little less a man; and she is a little less the woman she is. In the greater story of Man and Woman and their struggle to be united, this man and this woman are a little further apart.

When woman loves she can dissolve in herself most of the frustration caused by man's premature ejaculation. Nonetheless, any residual emotion becomes a part of the fiendess and will crucify him tomorrow. But her love cannot compensate for her basic unfulfilled need — to give up her finest female energies to her lover, to express her intrinsic female beauty, the divine fragrance which builds up continuously in every woman and which is behind man's need of her. Because of his default, she has to carry this unnecessary burden; and the pain of it is the deep grievance behind the punishing moods and emotional fury of the fiendess.

〜

Selfish sexual man normally uses the act of love to ejaculate, to release his pent-up psychic aggression. In his so called lovemaking he habitually uses the woman for his own sexual gratification.

In extreme cases of sexual aggression man can possess woman with a devilish sexual energy. He trains her to excite him to fever point, so that in intercourse she becomes a gyrating robotic performer. During the act he contains his orgasm by rigid mental control, a practised and efficient hardness derived from his sense of power over the woman. He enjoys being able to degrade her, to degrade love with excitement — a devilish pleasure. He enjoys the manipulation of her more than he enjoys orgasm. The woman, with a chronically excited vagina, lined with male sexuality, then becomes what she hates. She becomes twenty-five percent sexual male.

I said that the man in this case is devilish. But I must also say that no individual man is all devil. All men have their moments of being love. The devil is a psychic possession in the subconscious; and in that sense it *is* the man, but it is not the man all the time.

Man must learn to make love without being selfishly sexual. As he learns to love or enjoy woman without needing an orgasm to release his sexuality, he starts to love her rightly. He delights her — and delights in her — rather than aiming to excite her and himself. Man learns to make love rightly in this way by reducing his normal male level of sexual excitation. And he does this by cutting out sexual fantasy.

It is possible to fantasise about sex but not about love. In love the still image of the beloved is held in the consciousness. No movement, no thinking, just the energetic presence of the love. When fantasy takes over, and erotic moving pictures take on a life of their own, love is deserted for the male-induced mentality of the sex shop.

Woman as a rule does not fantasise about sex as much as man because sex is not as gratifying for her. It only serves to gratify the sexual excitement man has put into her. Woman knows deep down that love is not sex. Her main fault is that from childhood she fantasises about romantic love and daydreams of mythically amorous situations. The selfishness of man's actual physical loving of her collides violently with this entrancement. Very soon she subconsciously acquires emotions of disappointment, disillusionment and frustration with man's idea of love. But what can she do when experience shows her that there's nothing else but sex and selfishness? That love is apparently a dream? So she joins man in his fantasising, his dream, and leaves *her* dream behind. The suppression festers in her as doubt, fear, and in extremes a subconscious hatred of man for his failure or betrayal.

CONSCIOUS LOVE

*M*an can never be happy for long — until he has made sufficient love to replace his selfish attachment to sexual games-playing and sexual entertainment. Since world progress is his own clever invention to escape this responsibility, he has devised almost foolproof contraception methods (chemical: the pill; and surgical: vasectomy) to ensure the service of his own pleasure at the expense of love. The downside of this (there's always a downside to selfish pleasure) is the unstoppable burgeoning of the world population. The need to control the birth rate on the planet arose only because man lost sexual control of himself, releasing sperm when he masturbates outside the vagina and ejaculating inside as a matter of course.

When time and the world were very young, and man

and woman made love like gods, it was a great privilege to be present in a body on earth. Since man was responsible to love, or woman, the population was kept very small. Man did ejaculate in lovemaking, but very rarely, and the moment was determined by the divine intelligence, love itself, with which he was united.

Man and woman today can enter the consciousness of love, which lies behind the part of the brain that controls the genitals. This is done through right loving; by being the feeling in the vagina or penis; by not trying to stay aloof, or hold on to a separate identity. Then the two poles of love on earth, the masculine and the feminine, are united in the magical consciousness, the divine presence of their mutual godhead.

∾

There are two different energies of love; one in the upper body and one in the lower.

The upper body vibrates with a very fine energy, felt particularly in the solar plexus and if you are a woman, in the breasts. As this is the finest and sweetest of woman's psychic energies of love, the kissing of her breasts and nipples is extremely important. They require a very gentle and loving physical approach by man. Many men are greedy, grabbing and even violent in their fondling and kissing of the breasts. Instead of adding to the woman's loving response, this behaviour destroys the sensitivity in her breasts and she stops feeling the love in them. Also it adds further to her revulsion against sex and will influence her future response even to a loving and gentle man. The love in her breasts gives milk to the child and holds its beloved to the bosom without taint of sexuality. It can be felt as longing for the unattainable, yearning for purity and ideal beauty. It is the impulse behind the idea of platonic love. This is the upper pole of love.

The lower pole, below the waist, is focused in the genitals, although the energy of it is continuously present (and normally not discerned) in the lower back, base of the spine, thighs and legs. If you are very still, you will eventually locate the distinct feeling of this energy. When perceived without emotion or sexual associations, the lower energy is felt to be just as pure as the higher love, but the sensation is more grainy or tangible. This energy, rising out of the earth itself, is pure vitality or life-force, before emotion as sexuality or sentiment enters it.

In very few men or women is the body above the waist integrated with the body below it. The function of man or the masculine principle is to unify these two poles of love in woman. Although there is the same lack of integration in him, he only has to focus on loving and delighting his partner; everything will flow from that, including the resolution of his own sexual disharmony and frustration.

When woman's whole system flows freely she is fulfilled with divine love. For this union of the upper and lower in the body, the ideal and the earthy, the unattainable and the attainable, produces the single current of divine love, a radiant golden energy. And when this is fully achieved, women are reunited with the original woman — physically, psychologically and spiritually. Her discontent vanishes and she is no longer dependent on any external activity for a sense of fulfilment or purpose. She may still engage in her work or art, or motherhood, but is no longer attached to her pursuits as a need. All possible fulfilment is in this one yoga or union.

As you can see from the world around you, it is rare indeed for a woman to be in this natural, original state. Yet woman's total sexual motivation is to make this divine connection through man. Even her desire to produce children is secondary. Because the divine connection is so rarely made, woman today is not really herself. She stays mostly in the romantic upper body, yearning for the unattainable; and periodically or promiscuously engaging the lower body in sex, in a futile endeavour to make the connection. It evades her, so she remains virtually two people, divided in herself, until quite often in disillusionment or old age she cuts off from sex and lives a half-life of idealised love. In some extreme cases she will be called 'frigid'. In other cases her cutting-off will exacerbate the tendency in man towards impotence.

To see through the sexual problems associated with this lack of integration, you have to see that in divine or real love the 'union' is not only of man and woman and their two bodies, but of each of them within their own bodies.

The tendency in woman to remain in her yearning makes her vulnerable to sentiment and false romance. True romance is not a passing thing. It is not a box of chocolates, an anniversary remembered, or sweet words, pretty things and beautiful evenings together. Indeed these are a part of the romance of living; but so is death, which robs woman of all her romantic illusions.

In the romance of living, you can't have the good without the awful shock. True romance is the myth of life, the stupendous adventure of man and woman discovering together through love, through each other, that there is no death, no end to life or love that does not hold or fear.

❧

Now let's look at what happens at the moment of orgasm.

Orgasm is a part of lovemaking. But all too often orgasm is an emotional end. And lovemaking has no end. True lovers go on and on, making love until finally, perhaps hours later, the man ejaculates naturally and consciously. Or they pull apart and make love hours later, or the next day and the next and the next, without the man necessarily having to come.

The emotional end to orgasm is a let-down, a period of post-coital sadness or depression. Before the troublesome emotions of the self are dissolved, physical intercourse stirs deep emotions of self-doubt. But know that this is so and is actually part of the spiritual process of facing yourself in order to know yourself. Most people miss the significance of post-coital depression and identify with it instead of gradually detaching from it.

Orgasm is well and truly beneath the moment to moment beauty and purpose of lovemaking, but it will happen rightly for both of you, without producing emotional traumas afterwards, if you are present enough to concern yourselves only with making love.

For man to come before he's made enough love, before he's gathered his partner's divine energies, is gluttony.

In woman, coming is easy and natural, sweet and becoming, if she can transcend her self-protectiveness and if only her partner can give her the chance to be natural and come naturally. But man is often too selfish. Down through the ages in his sexual greed he has taught her, tricked her, into chasing the orgasm, to divert attention from the lovemaking he cannot give her.

You cannot be aware of the sensation of love if you are chasing an orgasm; or, in the case of a man, if you are trying to delay one. And a woman who believes orgasm is important but can't seem to have one, will feel deprived or guilty; and she might give up. Many women have turned away from lovemaking because they confuse love with orgasm. And they turn their backs on the real wonder and glory of love.

When woman stops trying to make love and is no longer lured or fooled by orgasm; when she refuses to have a greedy penis inside her and is pure and present herself in lovemaking, with not one thought in her head, the orgasm can come — naturally and effortlessly. It just happens beautifully, through the power of the loving penis deep inside her. The orgasm comes of itself, without either partner wanting it or trying for it; or it doesn't come, and that's no problem.

These days a woman can have an orgasm and hardly feel it. The consciousness of love in very many women has actually left the vagina. It is so riddled with past, with tension and emotion, that women can't fully get their awareness into it, especially up near the cervix. The vagina has been desensitised there, and it's getting worse with every generation.

Woman generally gets more pleasure and more sensation in the lower part of the vagina because man no longer has sufficient authority to get to the deepest (or highest) part or stay there in love long enough to do what he is supposed to do. Because he cannot reach the part of her that is next to her spiritual garden, where the true goddess of love resides, he has fetched her feeling (and her orgasm) down to the front and concentrated her awareness on the clitoris. He has done this in two ways — by persistent ejaculation immediately after entry, and by persistent stimulation of the clitoris with his fingers to compensate her for the orgasms she otherwise does not have. He has made clitoral satisfaction, clitoral compromise, the prize of lovemaking. She knows it is not love. But what else can she do? What else is there?

Because of man's failure to love her properly, she will masturbate on the clitoris as man taught her. If she were loved she wouldn't do it. Without man's influence she doesn't have the same compulsion to masturbate as he does in the relief of his sexual aggression. She got the habit from him.

Only the penis can really make love with woman,

not the fingers or any other device. Only man's living penis is designed to serve her in the vagina. Only a selfless, passionate, patient, loving penis can put the orgasm back where it should be — where orgasm happens naturally; where if it doesn't happen there is no disturbing emotion; when she knows by the sensation, the consciousness, in her vagina, that she is being loved.

Eventually, through loving woman, a man's hands become like his loving penis. His whole body becomes love and woman will recognise this if ever she encounters it. Then his hands can love her in loveplay as her needs require.

This cannot happen until man, through years of right practice of love, has developed and realised his psychic senses. The psychic senses are behind all the physical senses and are far finer and perceptive. As man learns to love the smell of woman he starts to actuate his psychic sense of smell. The same with his lips. As he kisses her body with increasing love — her hair, her skin, her breasts — his lips are endowed with a new dimension of communication. The same with his touch; it becomes a harmony, a flow.

Finally he realises the whole psychic sense of sense.

This is one sense instead of five and his whole body becomes that refinement of powerful and penetrating love. Then, even his presence communicates love.

For man and woman to make love beautifully and divinely requires a fundamental change in the penis and the vagina; or more specifically, in the part of the brain that controls them. The penis and the vagina have to be freed from the brain's ignorance of making love. They have to be consciously liberated from the emotion or unconsciousness of the past, from all the habits and misconceptions gained through attachment to past experience.

Your body doesn't have to learn how to make love. It makes love naturally, given the chance. But your attachment to past experience gets in the way. This emotional attachment is your self — the emotion of what you like and don't like, and all your attempts to repeat the pleasures and avoid the pain of past encounters. So your self can't learn to make love. Instead you learn to look after yourself in normal lovemaking. You learn how to both protect and project yourself, safely and astutely. This self-consideration turns love into sex.

You can't protect yourself and make love. You can't hold back in any way. But that's how men and women make love these days. Their experience has taught them to be cautious — not to give all or they might lose something, might get hurt. Fear is abundant. So they play safe. They don't know how to give all any more. It's been forgotten.

People in love so frequently feel the rending impulse to give everything, to want to tear themselves open — and yet they can't. You must have had that feeling at some time. It's your self you want to tear open and be rid of, the blockage that blocks your love in your natural body.

Would you be able to give your lover everything — now, this moment? The honest answer is no. You have the chance each time you make love and you haven't managed it yet. Or have you? You may feel it does happen sometimes, or nearly happen, but there's always a chance that perhaps you won't be able to give yourself completely. There's no chance, no perhaps, in love.

Lovemaking these days is a compromise, the acceptance of the best that can be hoped for or done in the circumstances. And it produces at best the best feeling that can be hoped for from compromise, and that is 'satisfaction'. That's like being drugged. You'll notice it puts you to sleep after lovemaking. It is personified in the world by the man-made god of love — orgasm. Man is orgasm mad and now woman, the goddess of love herself, infected and inflamed by this male madness, worships man's phony god. As if coming were a sign of love. Any animal can be made to come without a sign of love. But you can't make love without love.

So let's not fool ourselves or be fooled any longer. If you want an orgasm, go and masturbate. If you want love, stay with this way of love. Persevere, and the necessary fundamental change in the brain will eventually be made. The fundamental change can only be brought about by learning to become conscious in love, by making love for love and not for your self. This means being both psychologically and spiritually present during the act of lovemaking and preliminary loveplay.

First, what does it mean to be 'psychologically present'?

Because of the massive accumulation of past or unconsciousness in every body, you normally make love in a subconscious dream state. What happens is that rising sexual feelings excite the accumulated past experience of sexual pleasure in you and draw your attention or awareness back into the past as a mood, image or fantasy. Immersed in that past, you cut off as a conscious being from the love your body is making in the present. Psychologically you are absent from the event, no longer really with your partner. You have drifted off into a world of your own. You must have observed this in your lovemaking, possibly in yourself and particularly in your partner.

Everyone making love is consciously present from time to time. In those moments you may notice that your lover is in a self-contained private euphoria. He or she is clearly absent. It's like talking to someone whom you know is not listening any more. So rather than remain alone, out in the cold, you get back into your own personal dream state as quickly as possible, so that you too can lose yourself with erotic imagery in dreamland.

The purpose of lovemaking is to be present together in conscious physical union as man and woman. But your normal lovemaking is self-orientated, self-indulgent and self-gratifying; you are dreamworlds apart. In effect, you have both borrowed the other's vagina or penis to make love to your own emotions, your own past. In such an insulated encounter, how could there possibly be a conscious, timeless union of the male and female principles? Because more emotion is being made than love, and since emotion is invariably isolating, such lovemaking gradually pushes the lovers apart. They get tired of each other and the magic vanishes. Lovemaking becomes habitual, a duty. Or it is an emotional release like an outburst of anger. Misunderstanding, discontent and restlessness grow.

The existence of emotion or past in the genitals dramatically reduces the sensation and the pleasure. The more emotion or past, the more the feeling of love is numbed, and the more distant the perception of love's significance. Since every penis and vagina is more or less infested with selfish emotion, no one suspects that the delicious sensation normally felt in lovemaking has already been deadened and is distorted. Therefore no one looks for the joy that is naturally available in divine and selfless love; it's too unbelievable, too far outside the normal experience. It is towards this extraordinary, original state of being that I am endeavouring to lead you.

When the penis and vagina become free of emotion they make ecstatic love. The sensation and perception is so heightened that at first there seems the possibility of losing consciousness because the pleasure is almost unendurable. As the process continues, the awareness is of being completely present as the consciousness of the divine love being made. There is no limit to the expanse of being and joy and the immediacy of the spirit that is known to be the union. It is being in the divine presence, a union of each other. And because it is love alone that is being made, and not emotion or imagination, and as love unlike emotion or orgasm has no end, the same rapturous physical and spiritual delight is present in all subsequent lovemaking together. It does not vary. It has only ups and no downs, no moods, no confusions, no emotional disasters. It only gets better, finer, more divine and more real, more conscious and more present; and the perception of love, godhead and eternal purpose becomes more wondrous, more sublime until ecstasy becomes beauty.

As by now you will appreciate, this does not happen easily. A good deal of emotional and intellectual dying has to be done. It takes a lot of work on yourself, and together. But the wonder of it is, it can be done.

I have been describing what it is to be psychologically present in lovemaking. To understand what it is to be 'spiritually present' you have to understand the penis and vagina spiritually. For both are spiritual organs and together are the means of all love on earth.

If love is God, if love is our own godhead or the excellence of life, then the penis and the vagina are the means of that excellence. Every man and woman, every perception of love and beauty on earth, arises from the union of the penis and the vagina. Even homosexual love is a misapplied attempt to get back to the divine state where the male and female principles themselves are united — the state of union that transcends persons and personal love.

To make love properly man has to learn to be his penis during the act, to surrender to its greater intelligence instead of forcing his inferior, sex-obsessed emotional mentality upon it, with the result that the penis can't do the job it's supposed to do. The penis is the finest perceptive organ and instrument in the male body. It has a consciousness and awareness of its own. It is the positive, active organ of love on earth. It knows exactly how to make love and what to do inside the vagina. Even in normal unconscious intercourse the penis-consciousness can occasionally take over and the lovemaking is surprisingly good and right; but that of course is the exception because the penis is normally used as an instrument of gratification for the man's emotional aggression and the woman's self-forgetfulness.

The vaginal cavity represents the emptiness in woman, her eternal longing to be filled with love. The penis stands for the only love that can fill it and until the penis is there, man and woman cannot be content. The penis inside the vagina symbolises the filling of the enormous gap that has developed in time between the two sexes — the gap that created the world and through which the world continues to come into birth. The vaginal channel into existence is then symbolically sealed. The cavity and its missing mass have found each other and are complete.

When the act of union is complete, the search of the male and female wanderers in existence is at an end, or the need for existence is at an end. But life as birth and death goes on; for even in union the penis and vagina are doomed to separate. Above the place of union is the womb, and will of creation. The womb or will, the source of existence, will not allow man or woman to rest for long together on the face of the earth. The womb or will can never be filled as the vagina can, for the womb demands birth and existence. So even as man and woman, penis and vagina, find rest and completion in each other, the womb sucks into itself the seeds of life — and another restless particle of life, another penis or another vagina is born.

∽

Earlier I mentioned foreplay and loveplay. I want you to understand that foreplay is not loveplay. Foreplay is what people do to get each other excited before the physical act. It stirs fantasising in the man and emotions of past sexual excitation in the woman. Foreplay, as the word indicates, is the caressing and working up that happens beforehand — before the sexual act. It implies something to look forward to that's not present now.

Loveplay, on the other hand, is sufficient in itself. It is love and love is the same in whatever way it is practised. There is no looking forward because what is happening or being done is simply love now. If the sexual act follows, the quality of the love remains the same, although there may be a seemingly greater intensity.

This means that in lovemaking, just as in loveplay, there is no looking forward to say, an orgasm or an end. It is a continuum of moment to moment pleasure of being that has no future and certainly no past reference. Any past or future reference would be a thought. And in loveplay and the act of making love there cannot be any thought. If there is it's not loveplay, it's foreplay; and it's not lovemaking but sex.

Two things operate in the interaction of man and woman: the reality of the body and the unreality of the emotional self. Due to the sexual bias of society today most men and women are so possessed by their emotions that they never make a real connection with the actual sensation of the body. They've lost the power to distinguish between body and self, or love and sex. So for most people there's no distinction between foreplay and loveplay; sensual stimulation is the same as sexual excitation.

In foreplay people excite their self or emotions. This selfish excitement is not sensory, not actual. It is a stirring up of past emotional experience and anticipation. There is no excitement or anticipation of the future in the body. The body is stimulated by the presence of love but that stimulation does not have excitement in it.

Similarly in right lovemaking when orgasm occurs it is not exciting. It's a pure sensory intensity, not an emotional one. But most people emotionalise the sensation by interpreting it through their feelings. This is usually much less pleasure than they would actually receive through the direct sensation. They drink the water but miss the wave. This makes them discontented.

As I've said, love is actually only made between the penis and the vagina. Love made has a very profound function. It actually reduces the excitement in the subconscious or self. As you continue the process of making love, engaging in a minimum of foreplay, you will reach a stage of knowledge that you are no longer as excitable or projective as you were in the beginning. A demonstration of this will be a noticeable decrease in both of you in what was once considered normal emotional behaviour. Accompanying this will be a growing sense of stillness and peace and an increasing subtle detachment from worry and anxiety in the everyday life. As this happens it is possible you may engage in loveplay. But loveplay, you should know, is the rarest state of communication on earth.

I'm now going to speak about fellatio and cunnilingus. But again I must stress that these forms of loveplay lose their profundity as a means of love if they cause excitement at all or any fantasising in the man or woman.

It's all a matter of consciousness, of being more conscious. Consciousness means absence of excitement, absence of wanting and trying, absence of projection, absence of self. In absence, consciousness remains. Consciousness is the power to register what's happening through the senses or body without using past experience to interpret it. This means that love starts to disappear as a feeling and is replaced by the direct sensation or knowledge of pleasure, a very rare state indeed. The way most people are today, the sensory pleasure is interpreted through the past and is therefore not conscious or immediate.

Consciousness converts the physical act into something profound and spiritually meaningful. Whereas lack of consciousness makes the act a coarser and more animalistic activity which produces all the emotional disturbances and conflicts you see within you and around you. The power of consciousness is always towards the realisation of God, the Most High, the non-existent and liberates the being from the old animalistic identification.

Consciousness is holiness because there's no self in it, no personal gratification or selfish motivation.

Consciousness is what this whole teaching of love is about. So I must now speak to you from the point of consciousness which is the God point or love point that you and everybody on earth are endeavouring to make real as your own being.

In consciousness, woman represents the holy shrine and man, the holy worshipper of that shrine. Woman's genital organ is the shrine; and the vital power in man's penis is the worshipper. So we find in the experience of being human the compulsive need of man to worship at the shrine. His greatest desire is to get down on his knees before the shrine, to have the guardian pillars or thighs of the shrine open to him and then, parting the curtain of the shrine, to gaze into its mystery. It's like the ark of the covenant.

The ark of the covenant was a wooden chest the Israelites of old carried around with them through the desert. It's supposed to have contained the tablets of the ten commandments, and after they disappeared, the scrolls of the Torah. The chest was lodged behind a curtain. Only the high priest was permitted to part the curtain and enter. And when he opened the chest and looked inside he found nothing. It was empty.

Man, when he looks into the vulva, the physical

representation of woman's mystery, sees the same — nothing. But the nothingness is the power of the communication — if he can only look and see without using his imagination or identifying with the old animalistic desire.

His next move is to experience the shrine with his other senses, to touch it, taste it, smell it and finally through his holy instrument of full penetration, to enter it. All this should be done in worship, that is in love that transcends every thought and feeling in the interchange of consciousness between the two. For as man looks and sees consciously so does the female part look back at him in consciousness. He is looking into the eye of God in existence. This is where man and woman as separate beings vanish and the mystical union of consciousness occurs.

In touching the shrine, man's fingers may find their way into the vagina. This should be with a conscious knowledge of why he is doing it. Animalistically he does it because he's unconsciously moved to and the act again serves to excite himself and the vagina with anticipation, rather than fill it with a sense of purpose or love now. To a man conscious of what he's doing his fingers are an extension of his holy penis. The fingers can reach places in the vagina which the penis cannot.

Their function is to stimulate the membranes and muscles of the vagina and through them the bones of the cavity. His loving fingers help to remove the substantive build up of tensional unhappiness that occurs in woman's consciousness which, unbeknown to contemporary thought, is mainly centred in her genital organs. It is her pleasure to receive such love, his pleasure to give it.

For woman the holy power in man, the mystery, is in and behind the penis. From infancy she is attracted to its mystery and curious to know more about it. In maturity she is drawn irresistibly to fondle the penis, to feel the power rising from deep within it and finally to take it into her through her mouth in an action of sheer love and worship of the power. If the man is excited and indulging in any kind of mental connection with what's happening, his lack of consciousness will go into the woman's brain and reduce her consciousness. His energy instead of reducing her thought and emotionality will actually add to both.

Woman is less given to fantasy than man and this is evident for her in the practice of fellatio. Given the power, and not the excitement of the penis, the woman knows a great stillness. Her mind and emotions are absent. She becomes completely absorbed in the direct communication. Her self disappears. Although momentarily she may become aware of what she is doing, her identification with the act becomes less and less and she enters the place of transcendent consciousness. Transcendent consciousness is registered as a vastness, a void, a blackness or from the point of view of existence, as nothing. But it is real, has a quality of joy and fulfilment, and can't be remembered as anything in particular.

I trust that you will keep reading this book and put what I have been saying into practice. Love or God can never be the subject of a philosophic exercise. Love or God is too real. Love or God is living and doing now — not speculating about it, not thinking about it. In this book I trust I have been real and down to the blessed earth so that love and God are truly served in your understanding; not only when you are making love but now, when you have the opportunity to be all the love you've ever made. For now is every moment.

By practising together to make love rightly, without self-indulgence, without seeking emotional satisfaction and self-gratification, you will draw closer to the realisation of consciousness or love itself, and the conscious, timeless union of the male and female principles as one ineffable divine presence, realised as your own reality, the sublime selfless spirit of love and life.

OTHER TITLES BY BARRY LONG

MAKING LOVE
This book is also available as two audio tapes and has been translated into French, German, Swedish and Spanish.

KNOWING YOURSELF
Written during the author's own spiritual crisis, this is a classic statement of self-realisation. The true and false aspects of the human being are separated so that we see ourselves more clearly.

TO WOMAN IN LOVE
Barry Long brings a profound message for every woman that her fundamental nature is one hundred percent love. Shaking every sentimental notion of love, these letters reveal the pain of woman today and the transcending beauty of her quest for union.

ONLY FEAR DIES
Unhappiness, though accepted as normal, is not a natural part of life. This book works to remove worldly attachments and reveals the way to freedom and the joy of being.

MEDITATION A FOUNDATION COURSE
How to meditate in the midst of a busy life. A straight-forward and practical course of lessons. You're in meditation from page one.

STILLNESS IS THE WAY
An entry into the inner world of advanced meditation. You become more and more still, as you open the door to reality.

WISDOM AND WHERE TO FIND IT
This introduction to self-discovery shows what we can do to face the truth through meditation and self-observation. Barry Long addresses the challenges we face in the spiritual life, the false nature of belief, the problem of choice, the question of suffering and the conflicts implicit in conventional morality.

RAISING CHILDREN IN LOVE, JUSTICE AND TRUTH
A radical and practical approach to the challenges of family life which shows us how to bring harmony into the home, educate children in consciousness and help them as they go out into the wider world.
Easy-to-read dialogues about matters of real concern to every parent.

THE ORIGINS OF MAN AND THE UNIVERSE
A work of immense vision which spans life and death to
tell the entire story of existence. A book capable of
changing your picture of the world forever.

All of the above are available from bookshops.

BARRY LONG'S MANY AUDIO TAPES . . .

cover a broad spectrum: meditation, consciousness, life,
death, truth, love and how to live the divine life.
Tapes dealing with love and relationships include:

BEING HONEST TO LOVE ~ How to radically transform
your love-life with the power of truth.

LOVE BRINGS ALL TO LIFE ~ The Great Art; a mythic tale
of love and how it can be realised between man and
woman.

BEAUTY AND THE BEAST ~ To learn how to truly love a
woman is the inspiring quest of a noble man.

BEING TOGETHER (ZUSAMMEN SEIN)

LOVE AND EMPTINESS (LIEBE UND LEERE) ~ Two tapes recorded at seminars in Germany, with consecutive translation, showing us how to keep love alive in relationships.

SONGS OF LIFE ~ Barry Long's story of life and love, told through his own songs.

These tapes are only available by mail order from the addresses below.

∾

Details of Barry Long's books, tapes and teaching programme may be obtained from:

THE BARRY LONG FOUNDATION INTERNATIONAL
via the following addresses:

ENGLAND ~ BCM Box 876, London WC1N 3XX

AUSTRALIA ~ Box 5277, Gold Coast MC, Queensland 4217

USA ~ 6230 Wilshire Boulevard Suite 251, Los Angeles, CA 90048 *or call* 1-800-497-1081